ALECA✳ZAMM
Travels Through Time

Read more about Aleca's adventures:

Aleca Zamm Is a Wonder

Aleca Zamm Is Ahead of Her Time

Aleca Zamm Fools Them All

ALECA*ZAMM
Travels Through Time

GINGER
RUE

Aladdin

NEW YORK   LONDON   TORONTO   SYDNEY   NEW DELHI

ALADDIN

An imprint of Simon & Schuster Children's Publishing Division
1230 Avenue of the Americas, New York, New York 10020
First Aladdin hardcover edition September 2018
Text copyright © 2018 by Ginger Stewart
Jacket illustrations copyright © 2018 by Zoe Persico
Also available in an Aladdin paperback edition.
All rights reserved, including the right of reproduction in whole or in part in any form.
ALADDIN and related logo are registered trademarks of Simon & Schuster, Inc.
For information about special discounts for bulk purchases, please contact
Simon & Schuster Special Sales at 1-866-506-1949 or business@simonandschuster.com.
The Simon & Schuster Speakers Bureau can bring authors to your live event.
For more information or to book an event contact the Simon & Schuster Speakers
Bureau at 1-866-248-3049 or visit our website at www.simonspeakers.com.
Jacket designed by Karin Paprocki
Interior designed by Hilary Zarycky
The text of this book was set in ITC New Baskerville.
Manufactured in the United States of America 0818 FFG
2 4 6 8 10 9 7 5 3 1
Library of Congress Control Number 2017960993
ISBN 978-1-4814-7070-4 (hc)
ISBN 978-1-4814-7069-8 (pbk)
ISBN 978-1-4814-7071-1 (eBook)

For my husband and our kids

CONTENTS

1
The Importance of Proper Footwear for Invisible Bridges / 1

2
Waiting (in Snazzy Pink Sneakers) / 15

3
Even Grosser than a Fungus Monster / 19

4
More Majestic than a Toilet / 32

5
Mystical Three / 41

6
The Coolest Bridge Ever / 46

7
Crossing into Whenever / 50

8
Spry and Resolute Aunt Zephyr / 55

9
Time to Wonder Up / 61

10
So Many Reasons Not to Do It (but Doing It Anyway) / 65

11
A Lack of Pizzazzy Chickens / 68

12
Gallivanting and Dillydallying / 76

13
Little Aunt Zephyr / 82

14
Finding Ford / 85

15
The Boss of Everybody / 88

✳ 1 ✳

The Importance of Proper Footwear for Invisible Bridges

I could hardly sleep. Ever since I'd turned ten, my life had been more exciting than coming home to find a dozen monkeys wearing overalls in your bedroom (which has never happened to me but would be awesome if it did, and hey, you never know). I had found out I could stop time just by saying my name, Aleca Zamm. That meant I was a Wonder, a person with a magical ability. I was like my great-aunt Zephyr and her brothers, who had also become Wonders when they'd turned ten.

Before I'd known that I was a Wonder, I hadn't thought there was anything special about me at all. But now here I was, feeling very special, what with my ability to stop time, my teleporting great-aunt, and my new friend, Ford, who could see stuff from the past and the future. Like, he could see this bridge we were going to try to cross. That was not something just everybody got to do!

When I had gotten home from school that day, I'd found Aunt Zephyr a complete mess, watching a soap opera on TV and feeling all loser-y about herself because she thought she couldn't Wonder anymore. But I had gotten her out of her funk by telling her that Ford had actually walked on the bridge only he could see, and she had promised me that we—meaning Aunt Zephyr and me—could try to figure out a way to see Ford's bridge and maybe even walk on it too. I couldn't think of a good reason to wait until the next day to try this, but Aunt Zephyr could think of three reasons.

First, it was getting dark outside by the time she finally agreed to my plan, and she figured that if we were going to try to make seven-year-old Ford walk all the way across a bridge, we ought to wait until it was at least daytime so that it would be somewhat less scary for him. I should also mention that the bridge we were going to cross didn't exist anymore. Also Ford was the only person who could actually *see* the bridge.

Second, Aunt Zephyr needed to rest

because her teleporting had been *way* jacked up and she'd had a hectic day of landing in places where she hadn't intended to go.

Third, none of us could drive to school. You'd think that a lady as old as my great-aunt would have a driver's license, but why drive when you can just think yourself some-where? She'd never bothered to learn how to drive a car, so we needed to wait for Mom to take me to school the next day, since the bridge we were crossing was just a few steps away from school. But that meant we also had to come up with an excuse for why Aunt Zephyr would be going with me. We had decided that we'd tell Mom that Aunt Zephyr was going to be giving a talk to my class about geography, because she had been everywhere in the world at least twice.

"I suppose it should go without saying," my mom said when we told her the excuse the next morning. "But you won't be mentioning to the children that you *teleported* to these distant lands, will you?"

"Oh, Harmony!" Aunt Zephyr chuckled. "Sometimes we don't tell people the whole story for their own good. Don't you agree?"

Mom did agree. She just didn't know that we weren't telling *her* the whole story. Because the whole story was that Aunt Zephyr would, technically, be lecturing the class about world geography, but nobody would hear it because time would be stopped and they'd all be frozen. But she would still give a short lecture, even if no one heard.

I did wish Aunt Zephyr had toned down her outfit, because I didn't think it was a good idea to draw attention to ourselves on a day when we were going to cross a secret bridge, but Aunt Zephyr rarely toned down anything. Not her outfits, hairdos, or even the things she said. She was wearing a dress that had multicolored sequins the size of pennies all over it. And as if the sequins weren't enough, the dress also had a lace collar and hem and big buttons down the front. She was also wearing a scarf in her hair and big hoop earrings and high-heeled shoes with fringe that looked like fireworks exploding.

"Why is everyone staring at us?" she asked as we walked into the building.

"Because you are wearing every color of the rainbow and you are shiny," I replied.

"I will have you know that this dress is

from one of the most famous designers in Italy," Aunt Zephyr said. "Obviously these children don't know fashion."

"Obviously they're only in pre-K through fifth grade," I said. "And obviously you are not in Italy but in Prophet's Porch, Texas. What did you expect?"

"Young lady, it is not every day that I attempt something as monumental as merging Wonder abilities. This occasion calls for something special!"

"You sure nailed 'special,'" I said. And I guess she had a point. Because we were going to try to do something probably nobody else had ever done before.

I mean, how many people do you know who have actually walked on a bridge from the past that no one else can see? Of course

Ford had been too scared to walk all the way across it by himself. I couldn't see the bridge at all, and when I'd tried to walk on it with him, I'd fallen. Not far, but enough to know that there wasn't a bridge there for me. But Ford had kept on walking, and to me it had looked like he was walking on air. I couldn't stand it. I had to walk on that bridge too and see where it went. So Ford and I had cooked up this plan with Aunt Zephyr to see if we could figure out how to make it so I could see the bridge too. But we had to get all three of us together at once to try.

"Hi, Aleca. Hi, Ms. Zephyr." It was my best friend, Maria. She stayed a few feet away from us, and I didn't blame her. The last time she'd been around Aunt Zephyr, my aunt had rubbed noses with her. Rubbing noses is a form of greeting in one of the countries that my aunt likes to teleport to. But Maria hadn't known that, and she had been pretty weirded out. (You would be too if a complete stranger with orange-sherbet-colored hair suddenly stuck her nose against your nose.)

"Hi, Maria," I said. "You're probably wondering what Aunt Zephyr is doing at school today."

Here we go again, I thought. I was going to have to make up a story to tell Maria. I couldn't tell her the truth, because Wondering was super top secret. We had to keep it secret because Aunt Zephyr said that Duds (regular people) might be scared of Wonders or bad Duds might try to hurt us in some way. So we couldn't tell anyone—especially not people who had a hard time keeping a secret, like Maria. Maria was the best friend I'd ever had, and I *so* wanted to tell her that I had magical powers, but Aunt Zephyr had forbidden it. I had to keep making up reasons for the strange things that had been happening around me, like why the principal's pants had fallen down or why two mean girls had had their hair suddenly glued together or why a bug had appeared inside a bully's mouth. Luckily for me, Maria didn't really have sneakiness radar. Otherwise she would have been onto me fast.

"I *was* kind of wondering," Maria admitted. She was eyeing Aunt Zephyr's getup, and who could blame her? "Wow, don't those shoes hurt your feet?"

"Yes, they absolutely do!" Aunt Zephyr

beamed at Maria. "And thank you for noticing! I do hate to suffer for fashion and not have anyone notice."

"Wait," I said. "You're suffering? On purpose? Why would you do that?"

"Why, vanity, of course!" replied Aunt Zephyr. "What other reason could there be? My toes are crammed into these things like useless knowledge in the brain the night before a big test. And every so often one of my calves has a muscle spasm that would knock a professional wrestler to his or her knees! But these shoes complete my outfit in the most spectacular of ways. Don't you agree?"

"I have some rain boots in my cubby if you want to borrow them," Maria offered. I was just glad that the discussion of shoes had distracted Maria from her original question, about what Aunt Zephyr was doing at school.

"Here, Aunt Zephyr," I said, gesturing to a bench outside our classroom. "Maybe you ought to have a seat and rest your calves and your crammed toes," I suggested. "Maria, I'll catch up with you in a minute."

Once Maria had left and Aunt Zephyr had hobbled over to the bench, I sat down beside her and whispered, "Your shoes really hurt that bad?"

"Terrifically," she replied.

"Aunt Zephyr, no offense, but what were you thinking?"

"I already told you. I was thinking about how beautifully the fringe accents my dress!"

"No," I said. "I mean, the whole purpose

of bringing you to school was to see if we could walk across Ford's bridge. It would be hard to walk across a normal bridge in those things, but this is a *magical* bridge! Don't you think it would be best not to have to worry about uncomfortable feet at a time like this?"

"Hmmm." Aunt Zephyr pondered. "I guess it was pretty silly of me."

"I'll call Mom and ask her to bring your sneakers."

"Nonsense! I wouldn't dream of putting your mother through the trouble. Besides, she isn't at home anyway. Remember, she had to take Dylan to that doctor's appointment today?"

"Oh yeah," I said. My older sister, Dylan, was having a wart removed. "I guess you could try Maria's rain boots."

"That was a nice gesture, but they'd never fit," Aunt Zephyr said. "Nothing to worry about, Aleca." She looked around to make sure no one was watching. "I'll just teleport home quickly and change shoes. I'll be back before you know it."

"But—" I began. Before I could finish my thought, which was that Aunt Zephyr's teleporting hadn't been very reliable lately, she was gone.

On the upside, her teleporting had worked immediately.

On the downside, there was no guarantee that she'd teleported *home*.

❋ 2 ❋

Waiting (in Snazzy Pink Sneakers)

See, Aunt Zephyr had been winding up in all kinds of places lately when she tried to teleport. She used to be able to think herself anywhere she wanted to go. But as she got older, her power became a little wonky. She took unplanned detours sometimes. Detours to places like Wyoming when she meant to go to the beach. Or to our roof when she meant to land in my room.

Since teleporting wasn't exactly foolproof

for Aunt Zephyr these days, I figured maybe I should call home to see if she'd answer. The first school bell would be ringing in a few minutes, so I had to hurry.

Just as I was on my way to use the phone in the school office, though, I realized that the office lady would want to know why I wanted to use the phone. Before I could think through what I would say, I heard Ford call my name.

"Aleca!" he said. "Where is your aunt? I thought we were going to the bridge first thing this morning."

I had to explain to him about her uncomfortable shoes. And then I wanted to change the subject so that Ford wouldn't panic about the whole teleporting thing. So I said, "Speaking of shoes, look! I'm wearing my new pink sneakers! I got them for my birthday!" I had put special plaid laces in them that were aqua and white. This made them have extra pizzazz and also meant that no one at school would have the same shoes as me unless they were copycats. And I figured the chances of anyone doing that were slim, because what is worse than being a copycat?

"Yes, your shoes are very nice, Aleca, but where is your aunt now?"

"I'm not sure," I admitted. "She kinda teleported back to my house to change her shoes. At least I hope that's where she landed."

Ford said, "Why would she risk teleporting on today of all days?"

"I know," I said. "But there's no arguing with Aunt Zephyr."

"You'll stop time as soon as she gets here, though, right?" he asked. "I need to see that bridge again."

"And I can hardly wait to see it with my own eyes!" I replied.

"Then it's settled," he said. "When time stops, I'll know that Ms. Zephyr is back, and we'll get on with it."

"Sounds like a plan," I agreed.

The bell rang, and Ford and I went to our classes. All we needed now was for Aunt Zephyr to show up. I hoped she would get back before I had to start doing math.

✳ 3 ✳

Even Grosser than a
Fungus Monster

But Aunt Zephyr didn't get back before
math. Or before language arts. Or even
before lunch.

As usual, her absence was a mystery that
could have been easily solved if my parents
had let me have my own cell phone. Then
I could have called Aunt Zephyr and asked
her where in the world (literally) she was.
But I couldn't exactly ask for a pass to use
the office phone to see if my aunt had

teleported safely home that morning!

I was so nervous, I couldn't sit still. That was why I asked Mrs. Floberg for the bathroom pass, even though everyone avoided peeing at school because our bathrooms were gross. Most of the time everybody held it as much as possible—even on field day, when we had Gatorade and snow cones. But luckily, Mrs. Floberg didn't seem to mind getting rid of me for a few minutes. Maybe because she had already told me five times to quit fidgeting.

I went out into the hall. I could hear singing from the music room and kids yelling in the gym. I was trying to decide which one I wanted to go watch for a while, because of course I wasn't going to actually go to the bathroom. But when I rounded the corner, Mr. Vine, the principal, who also happened to hate my guts, was standing nearby.

"Oh, hello, Mr. Vine," I said.

"What are you doing out of class?" he barked.

I held up the pass. "I'm going to the bathroom," I said. "To pee."

Probably that was more information than he required, but I wanted to be thorough. Teachers and principals always like it when you're thorough.

Mr. Vine sneered. "I don't need a full report," he said. "Hurry up."

I scooted down the hallway, and just before I went into the scary, dark bathroom, I looked back to see if Mr. Vine was still watching me.

He was. Ugh. I took a big breath and walked to just inside the door.

I guess there was a reason why Maria was on the swim team and I wasn't, because I couldn't hold my breath very long. Almost as soon as I got inside, I had to suck a gross lemon-and-pine smell right into my nostrils. You would think that smell would mean that the bathroom was clean, but it did not. The lemon-and-pine smell came from these little circular blue things that the janitors put on the floor behind the toilets. The things looked like hockey pucks and smelled like cleaner but did not actually clean anything.

There was barely any light in the bathroom, except for a pair of flickering bulbs above the black-spotted mirrors. Some sunlight came in from two windows near the ceiling, but it only showed the cobwebs and the dead bugs up there. The ceiling itself had those panels that sagged and turned brown when they got wet, and most of them were as saggy and brown as a grizzly bear's belly. Some of the brown stains had black outlines, which I'm pretty sure was fungus that was alive and growing. Maybe one day it would grow into an actual fungus monster and take over the whole school.

I knew I shouldn't think stuff like that. All my teachers and both my parents had said that I had a very "vivid imagination," which meant that if I thought too much about something, I could scare myself pretty badly. And the more I thought about the fungus monster, the more scared I got. I started thinking how maybe the fungus had eyes that were watching me. And probably while it was watching me, it thought that it should eat me so that it could grow bigger and take over the school a lot faster. I got a bad case of the willies. Then, all of a sudden, I could have sworn that the monster called my name!

"Aleca!"

It was a raspy kind of whisper voice, but stern. Like it was not kidding around and really wanted my attention.

I gasped. I was just about to run out of the bathroom and tell Mr. Vine about the monster when the voice spoke again!

"Aleca!" it said. "I know it's you. I saw your pink sneakers!"

The voice was coming from one of the stalls.

"Come here!" it said.

I was no dummy! I wasn't just going to walk right into a bathroom stall and be eaten!

I had never really given much thought to what a fungus monster's feet would look like, but I bent down and looked under the stall door anyway. I didn't see any feet at all.

"How come you don't have any feet?" I asked. "Are you a monster?" Maybe there was a rule that if you asked monsters a direct question like that, they had to tell you the truth. It was worth a try.

"Aleca, for pity's sake, it's me! Aunt Zephyr!"

"Oh!" I said. What a relief! "Well, why didn't you say so?"

So I pushed the door open and . . . you will never believe what I saw.

I'm not kidding. You will *not* even believe it. Are you sitting down right now? You need to be sitting down, because what I am about to tell you will *blow your mind*.

Aunt Zephyr was standing on top of the toilet!

And one of her feet was stuck INSIDE THE TOILET!

Ewww! Now aren't you glad I made sure you were sitting down?

"Aunt Zephyr! Get your foot out of the toilet!" I said. At least she was wearing comfortable shoes now. But I hoped they weren't her favorites, because if it were me, I'd probably have to burn them after this.

"Hmm. Get my foot out. What an intelligent idea," Aunt Zephyr said. She stared at me with a blank face. "And to think that all this time I've just been standing here enjoying myself."

That was when I realized that Aunt Zephyr was being sarcastic. Because no way would she have enjoyed having her foot in there. "I guess you're stuck," I said.

"Brilliant deduction," she replied.

"Well, why did you put your foot in there in the first place?" I asked.

"Obviously it wasn't my intent," she said. "When I tried to teleport back after changing my shoes, I didn't quite hit my mark."

"On the upside, at least you landed at my school."

"Yes," Aunt Zephyr said. "Eventually."

"Eventually?"

"There were a few . . . unexpected detours along the way."

"Where?" I asked.

"Well, first I landed with the Emberá tribe in Panama. I got a little distracted there because they were carving tagua nuts, and well, that's just something I hate to miss. Here. I made you a frog." She handed me a little carving of a frog sitting on a rock. It was pretty cool-looking and very slick and colorful. "I wasn't going to take the time to paint it, but I couldn't seem to think myself out of there, so I figured, why not paint while I waited?"

"And after that you ended up here?"

"Not exactly," Aunt Zephyr said. "There was also a brief stop in Las Vegas."

"Las Vegas!"

"It was most unfortunate," she explained. "I landed right onstage in the middle of a group of showgirls. I tried to join in with the high kicks—you know, just to keep from calling attention to myself—but I wasn't wearing the right outfit and the giant headdress, so I stood out."

I thought that was probably not the only reason she'd stood out, but I kept that thought to myself.

"And then you landed here?"

"Yes," she replied. "I'm sure those security guards who hauled me offstage in Vegas are still wondering how I managed to give them the slip."

"But now your foot is stuck, and you can't get it out?"

"Precisely. A little help here?"

I grabbed hold of Aunt Zephyr's hands and tugged as hard as I could. She would not budge. I tried a few more times, but nothing. Then I heard another voice. But it wasn't a fungus monster. It was Mr. Vine.

"Aleca Zamm, you've been in there a mighty long time, young lady!" he shouted from outside the bathroom. "Is everything all right?"

"Yes, sir," I called.

"Then it's time you got back to class," he replied.

Aunt Zephyr looked at me and nodded. "I'll be right out!" I hollered. "Or my name isn't . . . ALECA ZAMM!"

The bathroom lights stopped flickering, and the school became quiet. The distant singing from the music room and the yelling from the gym ceased immediately. I turned to Aunt Zephyr. "Now that time stopped, I'll go find Ford and see if he can help us get you unstuck. Just wait here."

Aunt Zephyr cut her eyes at me and added, "Very funny."

Oh yeah. It wasn't like she was going anywhere.

❄ 4 ❄

More Majestic than a Toilet

If you've ever wondered what the greatest feeling in the world is, I can tell you. It's stopping time and then messing with your principal just because you can.

When I turned the corner out of the bathroom, Mr. Vine had his right hand stuck out against the wall, leaning all his weight on it.

"How's it going, Ricky?" I gave him a couple of pats on the face like mob bosses do on TV shows. I said the "Ricky" part because Mr. Vine's first name was Richard, which sounded distinguished, but Ricky sounded like a kid, and it was fun to talk to Mr. Vine like he was a kid instead of having to be all respectful of his elder-ness. "You know, sometimes you just make this a little too easy." And even though I knew I should hurry up and go find Ford, I couldn't resist scooting Mr. Vine back from the wall just enough to make things interesting when time started again.

"That's actually pretty dangerous." It was Ford. He had already come looking for us.

"Aww, what's it going to hurt?" I replied. "It will be funny. When time starts again, he'll lean all his weight into the air and fall down."

"And probably fracture his wrist when he

does," Ford said. "His trajectory, combined with the force of his weight—"

"Are you saying I have to move him back?"

"At least give him something soft to break his fall."

I snapped my fingers. "Dog poop! Dog poop is soft!"

"Aleca . . . ," Ford said, sounding like a grown-up, as usual.

"Fine." I scooted Mr. Vine back so that he wouldn't fall down when I started time back up. "But don't think I'm finished with you, Ricky," I said.

"Where's Ms. Zephyr?" Ford asked.

"Right in here," I said, pointing at the girls' bathroom. Ford looked scared. "Nobody else is in there," I promised him. "Not even a fungus monster." He didn't ask what a fungus monster was, because obviously he had thought about them before too.

When we reached Aunt Zephyr, she said, "Thank goodness."

Then Ford said, "Why is there a tree in the girls' restroom?"

"A what?" Aunt Zephyr and I asked.

"I suppose I'm seeing something from the past or future again," Ford explained.

"Oh!" I replied. "I guess that back before they built the school, a tree was right there."

"A big one," Ford said. "It's . . . majestic!"

I hated to break it to him that the majestic tree had been cut down and that in its place was a very un-majestic toilet bowl, but somebody had to. "Ford, there's no tree. Not in our time period, anyway. There's a toilet there. And Aunt Zephyr's foot is stuck in it."

We explained how Aunt Zephyr had gotten into such a mess. Then, since Ford had known so much about the way Mr. Vine would fall and break his wrist, I asked him, "Is there a mathematical formula or something for unsticking her foot?"

Even though he couldn't see the toilet bowl, Ford pulled at Aunt Zephyr's leg and said, "Haven't you thought of the most obvious solution?"

"Sawing off her foot?" I asked.

"Aleca!" Aunt Zephyr shrieked.

"Of course not," Ford said. "She should teleport somewhere else."

"Weren't you listening when we told you how I ended up here?" Aunt Zephyr asked. "My teleporting is out of whack! I can't do it!"

"Sure you can," Ford said. "You're probably just nervous. Your confidence has been shaken. Take some deep breaths and try again."

While we waited, Ford and I played a game of tic-tac-actual-toe in the floor dirt with the toes of our shoes, but Aunt Zephyr stayed put.

"Let's both give her a big tug and see if that helps," I offered.

"I can't see the angle of how her foot is caught, though," Ford said. "We might fracture a bone."

I sighed. I thought Ford should be a bone doctor when he grew up. He sure thought about fractures a lot. "Just tug," I said.

Ford grabbed one of Aunt Zephyr's hands, and I grabbed the other. Just as we were about to tug, though, something strange happened—stranger than stopping time and teleporting, even. For a moment the toilet *disappeared*. In its place was a tree.

I was so shocked that I let go of Aunt Zephyr's hand, and the tree vanished. "I just saw the tree!" I said.

"You saw it too?" Aunt Zephyr gasped.

"You see it too? A sycamore tree?" Ford said. "At least a hundred feet high!"

We all looked at one another.

"Take my hands again, both of you," Aunt Zephyr ordered. "And no matter what happens, don't let go until I tell you."

We grabbed her hands. The toilet disappeared again. The tree was in its place.

38

Aunt Zephyr spoke calmly. "Now back away slowly." We did. Aunt Zephyr backed away with us, because there was no toilet there anymore for her foot to be stuck in. Her foot was simply on top of a tree root.

"Now let go of my hands," Aunt Zephyr said.

Ford and I let go. As soon as we did, the tree was gone and the toilet returned.

Aunt Zephyr shivered and started kicking her foot wildly. "Get. This. Thing. Off. Of. Me!" She kicked so hard that her wet toilet-y shoe flew through the air and hit the wall before falling to the ground. Then Aunt Zephyr stuck her foot in the sink and started squirting pink soap all over it and scrubbing like crazy.

"Obviously we are going to have to find

a teacher in this school with a size nine foot so I can borrow her shoes beforehand."

"Beforehand what?" I asked.

Aunt Zephyr grinned. "I think we just figured out how we're going to see Ford's bridge together."

❄ 5 ❄

Mystical Three

I loved a lot of things, but the sparkle in Aunt Zephyr's eyes when she got excited had to be in my top ten. And, boy, were her eyes sparkling now!

"I don't understand," I said. "What just happened?"

"You . . . the two of you!" Ford said. "You just—you just participated in my Wonder ability!"

"Yeah," I agreed. "But how'd we do it?"

"By holding hands," Aunt Zephyr said. "Didn't you notice that the tree appeared for us only when we held hands? It disappeared as soon as we let go."

I thought about this for a minute. "That doesn't make any sense," I said. "I held Ford's hand when he saw the bridge, but I still couldn't see it."

"Or touch it," Aunt Zephyr said. "But this time you saw the tree with your own eyes. And not only that. Couldn't you smell it? I felt the root under my foot. It was *there*, Aleca. If we'd held hands longer, we probably could've heard the chirp of birds nesting in its branches."

"I still don't see why holding hands made it happen today," I said.

"Three," Ford said. "It's a mystical number."

42

"Perhaps," said Aunt Zephyr. "Or it could be more than that."

Ford started sort of hopping up and down. "A conduit! You're a conduit!"

I didn't know what a conduit was, but I didn't want a seven-year-old to show me up. "Yeah," I agreed. "I'm probably a condo—a can-do-it—a . . . that thing you just said."

"Not you," Ford said, shaking his head. "Ms. Zephyr."

"A conduit, Aleca, is something that allows for a transfer. Like a pipe in a plumbing system, or an electrical wire," explained Aunt Zephyr. "Ford is suggesting that somehow his power ran through me to you."

"And also to you," I said. "So maybe you're just extra Wonder-ous."

"That's a good point," Aunt Zephyr said.

She stood up a little straighter and smoothed her hair with her hand like we were about to give her a Wonder award.

"Let's test that theory," said Ford. "Aleca, stand back, please." He put his hand out for Aunt Zephyr to take. I scooted away.

Aunt Zephyr took his hand. They stood there a minute. Nobody said anything.

"Are you speechless because you are both seeing something awesome?" I finally asked.

"No," said Aunt Zephyr. "We are speechless because absolutely nothing is happening."

"Except that my hand is getting a bit sweaty," Ford added.

"Aleca." Aunt Zephyr offered me her hand. I took it.

The tree appeared again.

"Now, Ford, you let go," Aunt Zephyr instructed.

Ford let go. The tree went away. Then Aunt Zephyr and I let go too.

"Mystical number three," Ford said.

"Let's try some different combinations to be sure," offered Aunt Zephyr.

So I got in the middle and we joined hands to see what would happen. Nothing. We put Ford in the middle. Nothing.

"Well, what do you know?" Aunt Zephyr smiled. "I'm a conduit!"

❋6❋

The Coolest Bridge Ever

Ford did not want to give up on his mystical three. "It takes all three of us. However," he said, "beyond the mystical nature of three, there is a certain logic to it."

"What's that?" I asked.

"You stop time," he explained. "I see things outside of time. Or I guess you could say outside of the time that exists at the present moment. But only your aunt has the ability to travel. Maybe that is why she is the conduit."

"But you were going to keep walking on the bridge last time," I reminded him. "Except I stopped you. So you were traveling all by yourself."

"Aleca, I 'traveled' only a few feet. Who knows what would've happened if I'd kept going?"

"We have to find out," said Aunt Zephyr. "Let's get me some dry shoes and head for Ford's bridge!"

After visiting four separate classrooms looking for the right size shoes for Aunt Zephyr's feet—and then one extra stop to Mrs. Swan's class because Mrs. Lang's shoes were too grandmaish even though they were size nines—Ford and I bolted out of the bathroom and out the school doors. Aunt Zephyr could hardly keep up, even in

Mrs. Swan's comfort-cushioned slides.

The bridge right in the middle of the soccer field. When we got to it, Ford said, "Isn't it magnificent?" He'd forgotten that Aunt Zephyr and I couldn't see anything except the field and the Dumpster over to the side. "Oh yeah," he said, remembering. He went to the other side of Aunt Zephyr, and we each took one of her hands.

As soon as we did, there it was: the most beautiful bridge I'd ever seen.

But there was more than just a bridge. There was a concrete guard rail on either side, leading up to the covered part of the bridge. The covered part was made of steel and was pretty far in the distance. There were zigzagging steel beams running along both sides of the covering, making it look like triangles were holding up the curved arch on top. Big cement columns supported the bridge where it stretched over brownish-green water.

Aunt Zephyr had a faraway look in her eyes, like maybe she was seeing something that Ford and I didn't. "I can't believe it," she said. "I simply cannot believe it."

"Let's go!" I said, pulling on her hand. "I can't wait to see what's on the other side!"

"Wait," said Aunt Zephyr. "Let's just take a moment. Something incredible is happening here, Aleca. This isn't the first time I've seen this bridge."

✳7✳

Crossing into Whenever

"How could you have seen this bridge before?" I asked. "This is the first time all three of us have seen it together!"

Aunt Zephyr smiled a strange smile and shook her head. "Aleca, I've seen a lot of things before. Not through any special power but just by being alive."

I didn't know what she was talking about. And I guess she could tell, because she explained it: "This bridge is a part of history, Aleca, and so am I."

"That's right!" Ford said. "You grew up in Prophet's Porch, didn't you?"

"Yes," she replied. "And this used to be the main bridge into and out of town. I've crossed this bridge many a time!"

"You mean they had concrete back when you were born?" I asked.

Aunt Zephyr rolled her eyes. "Yes, the dinosaurs mixed it up for us," she said sarcastically.

"What do you think all those structures from ancient Rome are made of? And modern concrete has been around since the late 1800s," Ford explained. "They started building bridges out of reinforced concrete in 1889."

I looked at Ford, amazed.

"I did some research," he said, "after I saw the bridge for the first time. I was trying to figure out how old it might be."

"If memory serves, this bridge was built not long after Texas became a state," said Aunt Zephyr.

I couldn't remember when that had actually happened—I think that was one of those things Mrs. Floberg had lectured about when I wasn't really listening. "Were you alive when Texas became a state?" I asked. She didn't answer, but from the look on her face, I was guessing it was a big no.

"They tore this bridge down after I moved away," she continued. "I remember coming home to visit and being so sad that it was gone. I didn't realize your school was right next to where the bridge had been."

"Well, it sure is a fine one," I said. "Can we cross it now?"

"I suppose I've squeezed about as much reverence as possible out of you youngsters," Aunt Zephyr said. She gripped our hands, and slowly we began walking on the concrete that led to the steel bridge.

I looked down at our feet and noticed that there were little clovers popping up through the concrete's cracks. "They needed some of that spray stuff Dad uses on weeds," I remarked.

"Good observation," said Aunt Zephyr. "This road wasn't paved until many years after the bridge was built. So the concrete is older than the bridge, and the cracks indicate even a few more years added to that, so that would put it . . . Oh, I just don't know! I didn't pay any attention to when they paved the streets when I was a child."

"But at least we can assume that we are in Prophet's Porch sometime during your childhood," Ford said.

"Hey, maybe we'll run into young you when we get there!" I joked.

Aunt Zephyr stopped us in our tracks. "I hadn't thought of that," she said. "Oh, Aleca! What if you're right?"

* 8 *

Spry and Resolute
Aunt Zephyr

I kind of wished I had kept that joke to myself. Because just when we'd finally started getting somewhere, Aunt Zephyr stopped walking.

I tugged at her hand gently. "This way," I reminded her.

"It's not a matter of knowing the way," Aunt Zephyr said with irritation. "It's what you just pointed out, and in the nick of time too! We can't simply traipse into the Prophet's

Porch from my past! What if I can't exist in two realms at once? What if I somehow damage my past self by trying to cram two Zephyrs into one realm?"

I didn't know what to say exactly, but I figured she had a good point. One Zephyr was probably about all any time period could handle. "Well, what are we supposed to do, then?" I asked. "Forget the whole thing?"

"Aleca," Ford cautioned. "Your aunt is right. It's possible that her theory of damaging her former self could have merit. Or what if attempting to exist twice in the same time period were to harm this Ms. Zephyr? It might cause a cosmic blow to her health in some way. And she's not exactly in the prime of her life at this point—she might not be able to withstand it!"

Ford hadn't meant to, but he had managed to say the perfect thing to get Aunt Zephyr to come over to my way of thinking.

"Are you suggesting, young man, that I might be too old and frail to do this?" She scoffed.

"I meant no offense, Ms. Zephyr," Ford replied. "But the facts are the facts."

"Here are the only facts you need to know," Aunt Zephyr said. "First of all, I may not be a young whippersnapper like you, but I am in excellent physical health for a woman of my age. And second, I am spry. And third, I am resolute. Do you know what it means to be resolute?"

I'm not sure if Ford didn't know or if he was too scared to answer, but he didn't say a word.

"'Resolute,'" continued Aunt Zephyr, "means I have made up my mind, and there is no point in trying to change it. I have decided that we are going to cross that bridge, young man, and we are going to cross it right now, and I don't want to hear any more lip about it! Does everyone understand me?"

Ford and I nodded. And I tried really hard to keep from grinning, because I didn't want to remind Aunt Zephyr that only a moment before, she had been the one trying to talk *me* out of doing this.

We walked across that bridge so quickly— so resolutely, you might say—that we barely even got a good look at the steel zigzags as we whizzed past. But I didn't mind. I couldn't wait to get across and see . . . whatever we were going to see.

Just as we got to the end of the bridge, Aunt Zephyr suddenly stopped again.

She took a deep breath. "Here we go," she said. We could see people and old automobiles in the distance. The cars were big and boxy, not curved around the edges like modern cars were. And their colors were brighter and prettier. Lots of blues and yellows instead of grays and tans. The people were all dressed up like it was a Sunday morning church service, even the kids, and the men and the women were wearing hats. "If memory serves, my guess is that this is right around when I was eleven or twelve."

"Oh boy!" I said. "This is the coolest thing

I have ever done!" And that was saying a lot when you are a girl who can stop time. But I meant it. "Come on!"

I tugged at Aunt Zephyr's hand, and we went forward, almost at a gallop. Which is probably why it hurt so bad when we smacked our heads.

❋ 9 ❋

Time to Wonder Up

"Ow!" I yelled. "What was that?"

Ford put out his noggin-rubbing hand
and laid it against a sort of window. It wasn't
clear like a window in your house; it was
more like looking through a thin freezer
pop after you've sucked all the flavor out of
it. "It's a barrier of some sort," he explained.

"No kidding," I huffed. "I figured that
out when I smacked into it." I looked at Aunt
Zephyr, hoping she had a better explanation.

"Hmmm" was all she had to offer.

"Ford, what's wrong with your ability?" I demanded. "What good is it to take us across a bridge to the past if we can't get through to the past?"

"I don't know," Ford said. "It's not like I've ever tried this before. Give me a break. I'm seven."

"Perhaps that's it," Aunt Zephyr replied.

"What's it?" I asked.

"Ford's only seven," she said. "We've discussed before how unusual it is that he came into his Wonder ability before the age of ten. Maybe he's only partially Wonder-ful. Maybe his power isn't fully realized yet."

That actually made a lot of sense. But it was still pretty depressing. "So we have to wait three more years to go back in time?"

"I don't know what the solution is, Aleca," Aunt Zephyr replied. "But I doubt it involves whining."

"I understand how you feel, Aleca," Ford said. "It's a letdown to come all this way, only to give up."

"Who's giving up?" I said. If there was one thing I wasn't, it was a giver-upper. "Let's just put on our thinking caps until we get an idea. I'm sure we'll come up with something."

We all thought awhile, and then . . . I had it!

"Mystical three," I said. "I stopped time. Ford saw the bridge. So now, Aunt Zephyr, you've got to do your part."

"What do you mean?" she asked.

"I Wondered up. Ford Wondered up.

Now you Wonder up," I explained. "We're here. The barrier is here." I knocked on the invisible wall that kept us out of the past. "And Prophet's Porch from your childhood is over there." Ford and Aunt Zephyr were both looking at me like they didn't know what I was getting at. "Your special Wonder thing is transporting from here to there, right? So get us from *here* to *there*. Aunt Zephyr, teleport us!"

✳ 10 ✳

So Many Reasons Not to Do It (but Doing It Anyway)

"Aleca, have you lost your mind?" Aunt Zephyr said. "We've never attempted group teleportation, even under the best of circumstances! If we're going to try that, the first time should be to a place on the map, not to a place in the past. We should try it in our own normal time period. And probably not when there are three of us. Just trying to take one more person with me might prove to be too big a strain. And all of that doesn't even touch on the most obvious of problems, which is that my teleportation has been on the fritz for some time now. You know that. Aleca, with all these crazy variables at once, my trying to teleport you and Ford and myself past this invisible barrier back into my own past is nothing short of—"

"Insane?" I said.

"I was going to say 'highly irresponsible,'" Aunt Zephyr replied. "But your word might work better."

"She's right, you know," Ford said. "There are too many ways it could go wrong."

But we all knew that no matter how many reasons there were *not* to do it, we were going to do it anyway.

Aunt Zephyr took a deep breath. "Fine. Let's just do it. But look, you two. No matter where we end up, do not let go of my hands."

Aunt Zephyr squeezed our hands, and we all shut our eyes. Then she whispered, with a little shakiness in her voice, "Here we go!"

✳ 11 ✳

A Lack of Pizzazzy Chickens

It worked!

Aunt Zephyr's teleporting was not wonky, not even a little bit. We went right where we were supposed to go, which was just a few inches away from where we had been. I turned to touch the invisible barrier we'd just crossed over with my free hand, but there was nothing there. "The window is gone," I announced.

Since she didn't have a free hand, Aunt

Zephyr leaned toward where it had been. "Well, I'll be swanny!" she said. "Swanny" meant "surprised" or something like that. I actually didn't know what it meant specifically, but when old people in Texas were shocked, they said that they would be swanny.

"Ford, can you still touch it?" I asked. Ford put out his hand too, but nothing was there.

"You know what this means, don't you?" Aunt Zephyr said. "It means we are actually one hundred percent in the past!"

"YES!" I shouted. I got so excited, I started to dance. And when I did, I swung my arm so hard that I accidentally let go of Aunt Zephyr's hand!

We all gasped because we expected the past to go away, at least for me and Aunt

Zephyr, but it didn't. It was all still there.

"How come everything is still here even though I goofed up and un-held hands?" I asked.

"Fascinating!" said Ford. "I guess once we get through the portal, the hand-holding thing is off."

"Cool," I said. "Now that we can roam free, I want to check out the town."

In the distance I could see what looked like Prophet's Porch's current downtown area, except not. "Is that the folk-art museum?" I pointed to a building on the corner. The outside of the folk-art museum in Prophet's Porch was painted all kinds of weird, and I loved it. On the side of the building there was a giant chicken in different colors, and the chicken's wings were made up of reflective shiny glass. That chicken had pizzazz. This building looked like it was in the same spot, but there was no pizzazzy chicken, just brown bricks.

"In your time period, yes, that's the museum," Aunt Zephyr replied. "But in this one it's Newman's grocery."

"Newman? Isn't he the one who tried to cheat your brother Zander, but Zander read his mind?"

"The same."

"Hey, I know! Let's go tell him off!" I suggested.

"You're the first person in history to time travel, and all you can think of to do is tell someone off?" Ford said. "Shouldn't we be righting the wrongs of history or telling people about vaccines or something?"

"Absolutely not!" Aunt Zephyr replied. "The last thing we want to do is try to alter history in any way! Haven't you ever heard of the butterfly effect?"

"Is that the thing Dylan and her friends do with their eyeshadow?" I asked.

"It's the idea that small things—even something as small as the flutter of a butterfly's wings—can have large consequences," Ford explained.

"And I suppose you've studied it in science?" I asked.

"No. I've read about it in sci-fi books and seen it in probably a hundred TV shows and movies."

"The point is," Aunt Zephyr interjected, "we don't want to do anything that might

72

change our own time period. We are here simply to observe. Got it?"

"Fine," I said. And really, it did seem fine. Because messing around with history sounded like more of a headache than I wanted to take on. I'd already had pretty much all the excitement I could take for one day.

"I must say, the past is remarkably hot and humid," Ford said. "Just like the present."

"Good ol' Prophet's Porch," Aunt Zephyr said. "So many things come and go, but you can always bank on our insufferable climate."

"If all we're doing is observing, let's observe somewhere that's air conditioned," I suggested.

"Good luck," said Aunt Zephyr. "Air-conditioning wasn't common when I was a child."

"You mean you didn't have AC?" I asked. "For reals?"

"Not in our homes. I mean, maybe a few rich people did. The movie theater was one of the first places to get air-conditioning, and some of the stores used it to attract customers. My family and I would go into town on Saturdays sometimes just to feel the cool air. The places that had it hung signs in their windows that said in big letters, 'AIR CONDITIONED!'"

"That is the saddest thing I have ever heard!" I said. "How did y'all survive?"

"Oh, don't be so dramatic," Aunt Zephyr chided. "Come on. I'll show you the signs.

You'll get a kick out of it. And then we'll—"

"Ms. Zephyr," Ford interrupted. "Aren't you forgetting something?"

"What?"

"The butterfly effect? And all that discussion about two of you existing in one realm and what might happen if your present self encounters your past self?"

"Not to mention that you don't exactly, um, blend in." I gestured to her colorful sequined dress.

"Oh." Aunt Zephyr sighed. "I got so excited, I suppose I forgot all that."

"There's only one thing to do," Ford said. "Aleca and I will have to explore by ourselves."

* 12 *

Gallivanting and Dillydallying

"Woo-hoo!" I shouted. "Let's go!"

"Wait just a minute," Aunt Zephyr cautioned. "Are you proposing that I just sit here on this bridge and wait while the two of you gallivant all over past Prophet's Porch?"

"Yes!" I said. "Come on, Ford! Let's gallivant!" I wasn't sure I had ever gallivanted before, but it sounded like fun.

"I don't think it would be wise for you

to wait here on the bridge," Ford replied. "Actually, I think you should consider hiding in the bushes over there."

Aunt Zephyr huffed, but I could tell she thought Ford was right. She didn't like it one bit, though. "What a treat this whole time travel thing is for me!" she said. "Don't be long."

"We won't!" I promised. I figured we would be gone just long enough to see what stuff was like back then. Because they did not even have Wi-Fi and probably for fun had to do stuff like churn butter or milk cows. "We just want to see what it was like in the olden days. Right, Ford?"

"The technology! I can't even!" Ford said. "You said there's a movie theater? Just think of all that vintage projection equipment!"

"Whatever floats your boat," I said. "Can we go now?"

Ford and I left Aunt Zephyr behind a big bunch of hydrangea bushes on the side of what was called a "motor lodge," which she said was like a hotel except everything was on one level. She made us promise not to dillydally, and I said, "Don't worry. We won't dilly or dally," and then Ford and I beat it out of there so that we could start exploring.

It was weird seeing the ladies downtown wearing hats and little white gloves and dresses when all they were doing was running errands. When my mom ran errands, she wore sweatpants and a big shirt that had stains on it from when we painted the living room a few years ago. Also she put her hair in a wad at the bottom of her head, where her neck started. But these women had put a lot of effort into their curls and had probably used gobs of hair spray and pins. It seemed like a lot of trouble, but I guess it was also kind of neat. I wanted to ask one of them how long it took them to get ready to leave the house, but I didn't want to butterfly-effect anything, so I just kept my mouth shut.

"How come you're wearing that?"

Ford and I turned around, and a little boy was staring at us. He looked about Ford's age.

I glanced down at our outfits. Ford was wearing some of those baggy shorts like basketball players wore, which was what all the boys at school wore. But he definitely stuck out now, because the boy who had asked was wearing blue jeans and a plaid short-sleeved shirt that looked like cardboard, it was so stiff. I, of course, was wearing my pink sneakers with the aqua plaid laces and a T-shirt that said TAKE A HIKE.

"Are you poor?" the boy asked. He pointed at my jeans, which were torn and had patches sewn on them for the sake of fashion.

"We're not from around here," Ford answered.

The boy scoffed. "I'll say!"

I was tempted to give this boy a good sock in the face, but I'd promised Aunt Zephyr not to butterfly-effect anything. I looked down at the tears in my jeans and tried to sort of smooth them over so that they wouldn't show as much.

"Can you believe the nerve of that guy, Ford?" I asked. But Ford did not answer because he was not there. "Ford!" I called. "Ford! Where are you?"

I looked all over, but he had vanished!

✳13✳

Little Aunt Zephyr

I wasn't sure what to do. Either I could look for Ford or I could go back to the hydrangea bushes and tell Aunt Zephyr that I'd lost him. I thought about how she would take the news that I had misplaced the only person who could get us back through the time portal. Then I decided I'd look around for Ford.

Think like Ford, I told myself. That was

harder to do than it sounds, because the thing that made Ford *Ford* was that he thought like no one else did. Still, I tried. I thought about numbers until my mind wandered, which wasn't very long. Then I tried to think about advertisements, but I couldn't remember any. Then I remembered what he'd said about the movie projector equipment. I snapped my fingers. The movie theater! It was just like Ford to get so excited about how something works that he'd forget all about the butterfly effect and have to go investigate.

I headed to the theater at the end of the block. Just as I started to walk through the doors, a little girl standing in line outside called to me. "You have to buy a ticket."

I turned to look. She was a skinny little freckled red-haired girl. I'd have known her anywhere.

Which was why, before I could think about what I was doing, I shouted, "Aunt Zephyr!"

✳ 14 ✳

Finding Ford

If you are ever time traveling and you don't want to disrupt things, it's probably a good idea to *not* call the childhood version of your aunt "aunt." Because it would freak her out.

"How do you know my name?" demanded Young Zephyr. "And why did you call me 'aunt'?"

"Oh—uh," I stammered. "I have a friend who lives in town who told me about you, and so I knew it was you, and also where I come from, we call everybody 'aunt' and 'uncle.' It's kind of like saying, 'Hey, bud!' Except it's 'Hey, uncle!' Or 'What's up, aunt?' It's just a thing we do."

Young Zephyr looked at me, all skeptical, and then said, "I was born during the day, but not yesterday."

And I couldn't even help it when I gasped and replied, "That is totally something you always say!"

Young Zephyr cut her eyes at me, just like she always did as an old woman, and said, "Who do you know in town who knows me?"

"Wow, you are really something!" I said. That was a thing I said when I was trying to get out of answering someone's actual question. "I've gotta go!" I yelped, and then I just ran into the movie theater, past a guy wearing a jacket that made him look like a hotel doorman in a big city. He tried to catch me, but I was too fast. I ran into the room where the movie was playing.

I looked up at the projection booth. "Ford!" I shouted. "Get down here! Now!"

And what do you know? He did.

✳15✳

The Boss of Everybody

I didn't have time to lecture Ford about wandering off, because we had to run out the back door to escape from Young Zephyr before she could ask any more questions.

When we got back to the motor lodge, I called toward the hydrangeas, "Come on, Aunt Zephyr! We have to get out of here!"

"What's your hurry?" Aunt Zephyr asked, crawling from behind the bushes. "She's not going to come after you. Her parents don't allow her to chase lunatics in the street."

I stopped dead in my tracks.

"How do you think I knew it was you when you stopped time for the very first time?" she asked. "I'd met you before!"

I thought back to when Aunt Zephyr had arrived at our house, right after I'd become a Wonder. She'd known somehow that it had been me who'd stopped time. I'd even asked her how she knew, but she'd been mysterious about it. Now it made sense.

"Then all this time, you knew I'd run into young you?"

"I wasn't sure when you'd fall into this particular day in history, but I knew it would happen eventually."

"You're not mad?"

"What's to be mad about?" she asked. "As

far as anyone in Prophet's Porch knows, two crazy children ran like hyenas around the picture show, and no one ever saw them again. I'm the only person you really talked to."

"There was a boy who asked about our clothes," Ford said.

"Yes, I know. Max Phillips. But he's a doofus. No one listens to him."

"Then you knew all along that we could time travel!" I exclaimed.

"No. I knew all along that *you* could time travel. Up until your birthday party, I didn't even know Ford existed. And I didn't know that he and I time traveled with you."

"So when did you—" I began. But Aunt Zephyr cut me off.

"We can talk more about this when we get home," she suggested. "I don't want to

90

leave time stopped any longer than neces-
sary. Let's cross back over the bridge."

"Yes," said Ford. "The past is a nice place
to visit, but I wouldn't want to live here."

Aunt Zephyr looked back at the old town
and sighed, like maybe she didn't totally
agree with Ford.

We walked back across the bridge, and at
the end of the walkway, I stretched my arm
just in case. If there was an invisible barrier
on the present side like there had been on
the past side, I didn't want to find out about
it by whacking my head again.

I didn't feel anything. And even worse,
I didn't see the ugly green Dumpster or
my school or anything at all from my time
period. Just two-lane roads, gravel pathways,
one-story buildings, and a lot more trees

than there were in my time in Prophet's Porch.

"I can't see the present!" I exclaimed. "It's still just past stuff! And I don't see the barrier thing either! Does that mean we could be stuck here forever?"

Nobody answered me, which I took to be a big fat yes. I thought about what it would be like to stay in the past forever, with no Mom, Dad, Maria, or Dylan. I figured I would miss even Dylan eventually.

"Oh no!" I wailed. "We are doomed! Legit doomed!"

"You don't see it?" Ford asked.

"See what?" Aunt Zephyr and I said together.

Ford made his hand into a fist and did a knocking motion. "And you also don't hear it?"

"Hear what?" Aunt Zephyr said.

"The barrier. It's right here," he explained. "And through it I can see our school."

"You can?" I asked.

"Yes," Ford replied. "Join hands again." We did, with Aunt Zephyr in the middle.

And there it was.

When our hands were joined, I saw what looked kind of like a painting hanging in thin air. A big painting, about as tall as my dad and just as wide. (As wide as it was tall, I mean. Not as wide as my dad, who is actually not very wide at all.) All around the "painting," I could still see the old roads and buildings. "This is so super weird," I said. "But let's talk about it later. Right now I'd just like to get back." I'd actually be glad to smell the Dumpster again just because it would mean that we were back home.

But just as we clasped our hands more tightly and were about to go through the time window, something very strange happened. Everything changed. It was like someone had switched the channel on a television. The bridge and the trees and everything else from the past were gone.

Under our feet was a street made of some sort of silvery substance. Cars were flying past us. Flying! I don't mean "flying" like "going really fast." I mean they were actually flying in the air! And there were big shimmery buildings that had screens all over them that would change advertisements every few seconds. All the advertisements had something to do with the word "Zella." Zella cola, Zella flying cars, Zella perfume and purses.

"What's happening?" I asked Ford and Aunt Zephyr.

They both looked just as stunned as I felt, but Aunt Zephyr managed to say, "I believe we have hit a time travel glitch of some sort."

People glided past us on little contraptions like scooters, except they didn't actually touch the ground.

Aunt Zephyr let go of our hands and grabbed hold of a man zipping past. "Excuse me, sir," she said. "We're new to Prophet's Porch, and we were wondering—"

"New to where?" the man asked.

"Prophet's Porch," Aunt Zephyr replied.

"You must be lost," he said. "You're in Zellaville, the capital of Zellaland."

"Zellaville?" Aunt Zephyr said.

"Zellaland?" said Ford.

The man looked at us like we were nuts. "Named for Zella Zamm, of course."

"Zella Zamm?" asked Aunt Zephyr.

"The most wonderful person ever!" the man replied. "Everything here, and everyone here, is dedicated entirely to Zella! Zella is our queen!"

"Queen!" said Aunt Zephyr. "In the United States?"

"Oh, the United States hasn't existed in quite some time!" the man said. "Where have you all been?" He gave us another weird look and zipped away.

"There's no more United States in the future?" I exclaimed. "That can't be!"

"She's a Zamm," Aunt Zephyr said. "And clearly a Wonder."

"What's her Wonder thing? Being the boss of everybody?" I asked.

"Yes," Aunt Zephyr said, with a tremor in her voice. "Mind control." Then she snapped back to herself. "Ford, do you see that portal anywhere?"

"Yes," he answered. "It's still in front of us, just a few feet away now." We all joined hands again. I sighed with relief when I could see my school through the portal window.

"Let's get home," Aunt Zephyr said. "Let's hope my teleporting works flawlessly this time." Thank goodness, it did. It was a relief to get back to our own time, away from flying cars and shiny buildings and all that Zella stuff.

"Now what do we do?" I asked.

"First, we keep our word about the world

geography lecture," Aunt Zephyr replied.

We went back inside the school to my classroom, where, of course, everyone was still frozen in time. Aunt Zephyr addressed the class: "The world has a lot of geography. Any questions?" No one moved, so there weren't any questions, naturally. "Well, that should about cover it. The world's most succinct geography lecture ever. Aleca, Ford, get back to where you were so that Aleca can start time again. Meanwhile, I'll go home and start some research into this Zella character. She must be a baby or a very young child right now, if she has even been born yet."

"Then what do we do?" Ford asked.

Aunt Zephyr sighed. "Well, I suppose we have to figure out how to stop her. Go on. Get going."

Ford went to his classroom. I had to go back into the bathroom so that I could come out when time started again. I was so shaken up by everything we had seen that I almost forgot to finish that little number I was doing on Mr. Vine. Luckily, I had some gum in my pocket. I quickly chewed it and stuck it to the wall. Then I did a quick square dance move around him because it was all I could think of for my time stopping dance. It wasn't my best work, but it's hard to do-si-do when you're worried about the future of your country.

When I said, "Aleca Zamm," I heard Mr. Vine shout, "Ewww!"

I came out of the bathroom and found that I had positioned the gum perfectly so that Mr. Vine had leaned his hand right onto it.

"What's the matter, Mr. Vine?" I asked.

"Someone stuck gum to the wall!" he replied.

"Who would do such a thing?" I said. "I'd better get back to class now."

Of course it was almost impossible to concentrate on any of the boring stuff Mrs. Floberg wanted to teach us that day. But it was especially hard when we had a lesson in US history, because Mrs. Floberg said that democracy meant that we didn't have a king or queen and that we the people ruled ourselves. It made me sad to think that someday in the future that wouldn't be so and that everyone would be ruled by Queen Zella.

Queen Zella, huh? I thought. *Not if I can help it.*